WORTH A THOUSAND WORDS

A Collection of Short Shorts

Angie Thompson

Quiet Waters Press

Lynchburg, Virginia

Cover design by Angie Thompson
Photo elements by Petr Oralov, Jan Kronies, Erick Zajac, Pietro De Grandi, zhengtao tang, and Sarah Le, courtesy of Unsplash; Sandy Torchon, courtesy of Pexels.com; AndrewLozovyi and mauro1969, licensed through Depositphotos; and Anatoliy Sadovskiy, licensed through DesignBundles
Sheep logo adapted from original at PublicDomainPictures.net

This is a work of fiction. Names, characters, places, and incidents are the products of the author's imagination or are used fictitiously. Any resemblance to actual events, locales, or persons, living or dead, is entirely coincidental.

ISBN: 978-1-951001-21-6 (pbk)
ISBN: 978-1-951001-22-3 (ePub)

Publisher's Cataloging-in-Publication data

Names: Thompson, Angie, author.
Title: Worth a thousand words : a collection of short shorts / by Angie Thompson.
Description: Lynchburg, Virginia : Quiet Waters Press, 2021. | Summary: Seven short short stories exploring the values of friendship, family, and faith.
Identifiers: ISBN 9781951001216 (softcover) | ISBN 9781951001223 (epub)
Subjects: LCSH: Short stories. | BISAC: FICTION / Christian / Collections & Anthologies.
Classification: LCC PS3620.H649 W67 2021

*To Grandma, who always wants to know
if I've finished another story*

*And for my fellow chronic illness warriors:
Broken is about you*

*Thanks to everyone who's offered feedback on these
stories over the years and especially to the ladies who
helped me with all of these covers, even if they did
end up in tiny thumbnails!*

*Special thanks to those who provided the prompts,
pictures, and ideas that inspired these stories:
KDWC discussions and contests (Anything and Broken),
Bethany (The Promise), Kate and Rebekah (Grit),
everyone who wanted more of Love Blind (Fish Tears),
and Hannah (The Deal).
(And no, I didn't miss one; I have no idea where
Only a Treasure came from!)*

TABLE OF CONTENTS

Anything

"Well, first off, I guess you should know Gwen's okay."

Anne-Marie shifted uncomfortably in the hard plastic chair, rubbing her sweaty palms on her jeans. It was so odd, this talking out loud to no one. Well, not to no one, but to someone who might not even hear her and definitely couldn't answer. How did Gwen keep this up for so many hours?

"If you're—um—really listening or anything, then I figure you probably—wanted to know."

She'd never had trouble finding things to talk about before. "Chatterbox twins" Ryan had dubbed them—her and Gwen—back when they were kids. When he could stuff a couch pillow over his head or escape to his own room to block out the dreaded girl talk. When he could actually hear them, and they knew it.

"So yeah. She's fine. I made her go home and get some sleep is all. She's got that huge stats exam tomorrow—which, I guess if you can hear me, you know all

1

about that, right? I mean, I know they said you can maybe hear things, but—I don't know—can you actually, like, learn stuff? Cause it would be kind of funny if, you know, all her studying out loud and you woke up a math genius or something. But yeah, that—and these chairs—well, I guess you could probably figure out she hasn't slept well. So that's why I'm here. Alone."

She was rambling. Hard. Probably making no sense, even if Ryan had been awake. But that was the whole problem. If he'd been awake, she could have found something rational to say. Could have gauged his reactions and adjusted accordingly. Wouldn't have been so terribly distracted by the awful stillness of his frighteningly pale face.

Talk about anything, they'd said. *It's the sound of your voice that matters.*

"I'm not even sure I'm actually allowed to be here, you know?" Anne-Marie instinctively lowered her voice and leaned closer to the hospital bed, casting a wary glance over her shoulder. "I mean, obviously they let me in, but—I'm pretty sure they think I'm your sister. Nobody ever said I was, but—well, you know, with a name like Harris, people always make that mistake. And that first day, Gwen wouldn't let go of me, and the nurses just rolled with it, and—I mean, I don't know if there really is a family-only rule, but—and it's kind of the only way Gwen'll sleep, if I'm here, so—"

She drew a long, shaky breath, pressing her lips together hard and blinking against a sudden rush of tears.

"Man, Ryan, stuff like this isn't supposed to happen to you! I can't help thinking, like, was there something we could have seen? Something we should have noticed? I mean, healthy, fit, active guys don't just—just collapse without warning, right? Except obviously, yeah, but—"

She buried her face in her hands, struggling for control.

Anything. Talk about anything.

"Okay, so the doctors say we couldn't have known, but—it just feels like we should have, you know?" The hot tears clogged her throat for a second, but she bridged the crack in her voice and kept talking. "How does your—your—best friend's brother—have a massive aneurysm and—I totally never knew it? I just—I mean, I guess—I want there to be something—if we could've seen it—if they could've found it before—"

This was all wrong. If Ryan could hear her, it wasn't her tears he needed. It was her voice. Her strength. Any normalcy she could give. She could do this for him. Be stronger than this. She drew a deep breath, forcing the tears back.

"Yeah, okay. Change subject. You probably don't need all that right now. What do you want to hear? Cubs swept the Sox. Last one went to thirteen innings. Did you hear that one? I played it on my phone. Gwen says it just doesn't feel right to be in a hospital room with you and not have sports on, so— But there's nothing on tonight. I checked. Except NASCAR, and you'd rather di—" The blood drained from her face as the word touched her lips, leaving her cheeks cold with horror. "Oh, man, Ryan! I did *not* mean that! It's so weird—the things we say, and then—just please, please don't ever take your life for granted. It's so beautiful and precious—even if—you're stuck in a room watching NASCAR."

The tears came then, bringing the blood with them and scorching her face with a furious blush. She could almost see the look Ryan would have given her if he could—baffled and uncomprehending but somehow ready to forgive and forget everything once she'd gotten hold of herself again.

"Okay, yeah, I'm a wreck. I'm sorry. I think it's just—I've been trying so hard to be strong for Gwen, you know? And I just—can't help starting the 'what if's, and—Ryan, if you can hear me, just please, please come on. Please be strong. Please pull out of this. I can't—I don't want to imagine life—without you in it." She reached over and clasped his hand, a liberty she hadn't taken since the very first day she'd sat with Gwen in this little room. "You—you always said the 'other Harris sister' could call you for anything, right? Well then, please. Please get better. For me. For Gwen and me. We need you, Casey Ryan Harris. We love you. We always have."

A breath of laughter found its way through her tears as a memory stirred, and the corner of her mouth tilted upward as she let go of Ryan's hand to wipe at her eyes.

"Casey, wow—how long has that been? Did you know I cried for hours the evening you told us you wanted to go by Ryan? I wanted to slap that Kaycee West for making you think it was a girly name. I would've done it too, for probably a month—I was so mad! I felt like—I thought I was losing a friend—like Ryan Harris would be a totally different person than Casey was. Weird, right? I don't know. I was nine. What can I say? But you've always—always been one of the most important people in my life. You know that, right? I didn't have a brother of my own, and—yeah, all of that. Except—"

Anne-Marie's eyes slid closed, and she pressed her trembling lips together as she drew a shaky breath.

Talk about anything.

"I'm—I'm going to hate myself for saying this when you wake up, but—I mean, yeah, you probably won't remember it, if you can hear it at all, and—but I'll always be wondering, and—yeah, forget it. Forget I said anything. It's just—"

Her throat and her fists clenched tight again as she fought for control, but the long days and nights of anxious waiting and anguished prayer had frayed the edges

5

of her closely guarded restraint, and the harder she tried to hold it, the more it seemed to melt away.

"I mean, yeah, I should totally not say it because you are going to make it, right? And it'll all just be awkward and weird, and I'd rather you never knew than to feel like that around you. But I just—if you don't—if—if God—wants you home—"

Anne-Marie's head dropped into her hands and stayed there for a long moment as quieter, softer tears burned her eyes. Finally, her voice came, a low murmur beneath the beeping and clicking of the machines that were Ryan's lifeline.

"Casey, you've never—never been a brother to me. I know you've tried, but—it's not your fault. I just—I just love you too much for that."

Her body seemed to crumple as her lips loosed the secret she'd guarded so long. The tips of Ryan's fingers brushed her cheek as her head came to rest next to him. She closed her eyes, briefly savoring the sensation, then planted her elbows on the edge of the bed and braced her head in her hands again.

"Okay. There, I said it. That's it. I'm not saying it again, but—now you know. Maybe. Or don't. I don't know. I don't even know if I want you to. But I just—I couldn't let you go—without telling you." She sucked in a long, painful breath. "Look, I don't care how weird and awkward it gets—I just want you back, okay?

Dunking me in the lake and stealing my french fries and pretending to be my brother—I don't care.

"Find some sweet, pretty girl that you haven't known since she was all messy braids and freckles. Like I've ever lost the freckles, right? Just find her and marry her and have a bunch of goofy kids I can be an 'aunt' to. I won't care. I don't. I just want you to live, Casey. Ryan. Whatever." She choked on an indefinable mixture of a laugh and a sob. "I'll call you Batman if it helps, okay? Just live. Please live. Please."

And the "other Harris sister" opened her watery eyes and turned them toward Ryan's face just as the dark eyelashes began to flutter.

BROKEN

"You can not be serious." I pinched the bridge of my nose hard enough to start it throbbing as Alejandro awkwardly crawled into the passenger seat and wedged his crutches in the gap between us. "There's no way I'm taking you in to work like this."

"It is too late, David." His soft Argentinian accent held out the first syllable in my name just a beat too long, compensating for the stress he naturally wanted to put on the second. "I have already told Callie I am coming."

"Then call her back and tell her you're not. You know what, I'll call her." I fumbled in my pocket and immediately felt the absence. Alejandro held up my phone with a pale shadow of his usual grin.

"How do you think I called her, *amigo*? Mine was smashed, remember?"

How could he grin over something like that? My hands trembled on the steering wheel, and I gripped it tighter.

"How are you going to hand out ice cream on crutches, hot shot? Are you sure they cleared you for a concussion? Because you're sure not thinking straight."

"I will maybe need more practice for that." Alejandro wrinkled his nose a little as he glanced at the crutches. "For today, I can sit and watch the register while Callie scoops the ice cream. This will not be hard."

"That's not the point." I squeezed my eyes shut hard, then blinked them clear and tried to focus on the road as I put my junker in gear. "You've got a broken leg, for crying out loud! You need to rest—like actually rest—probably for a week, and you're not even giving yourself a day."

"Since Mitchell quit, there is no one to take my place. I cannot leave Callie alone there with the cash box." His voice was low and serious, and he didn't bother to hide the pain lurking beneath it. Of course it would be Callie—five-foot, fuzzy-headed, spitfire Callie, who'd probably weighed a hundred pounds sopping wet before the chemo and who'd only missed one day of work through her whole round of treatments, even as her bandanas grew more and more flamboyant to distract from her skeleton-like appearance. And Alejandro the loyal-hearted was much too noble to leave her at the mercy of the neighborhood thugs. Which was the entire problem.

"And you're going to protect her how? Kick the thieves with your cast? Or hit them with your crutches?"

10

My nails bit into the skin of my neck as I gripped it, shooting a glance up at the light. An angry red glare pierced the dark of my sunglasses, and I looked away again.

"It will be all right, *amigo*. I will prop it up when I come home tonight, and sitting on a stool will not be hard."

"Of all the boneheaded stunts—" I caught myself just in time as my voice rose toward a shout and changed it to a hiss. "You were hit by a truck, Alexandro! They can close the place down for a day, for all I care. If you make it through an eight-hour shift, it'll only be because you're too stubborn to admit when you've bitten off more than you can chew!"

The road blurred and swam in front of me, and I scrambled to blink it back into focus as the glare from the traffic light shifted to green.

"David?" Alejandro's tone was suddenly soft with concern. "Something is wrong?"

"Aside from you refusing to use the brains God gave you? Sure, everything's fine. Why do you ask?"

"You only say my name so badly when you are very frazzled." The concern in his voice was thick, and I didn't dare glance over at him, even to rib him about where on earth he picked up these words. "Your head is worse? Should I drive instead?"

"For Pete's sake!" I nearly choked on the lump that rose in my throat, and my voice faltered. "No, you

11

shouldn't drive. You're in a cast, or didn't you notice? This rotten migraine nearly got you killed today. Driving you back is the absolute least I can do."

"Oh, David." Alejandro rested a hand gently on my shoulder. "Do not do this. The accident was not your fault."

"It was my errand. You think I can forget that?"

"And I am your friend. Why would you forget that? You did not even ask my help."

He was right; I hadn't, but the wave of relief I'd felt when I woke to find the note he'd left next to my switched-off alarm had made the guilt even deeper when the call came from the hospital. I fought back the stinging sensation pricking my eyes. No use making it even harder to keep them focused on the road.

"I am sorry you had to come for me." Remorse cut deep in Alejandro's tone, and I gripped the steering wheel so tightly I could have snapped it.

"You're sorry. *You're* sorry? Because I had to drive the five blocks to the hospital after you took a bus across town with what—four hours of sleep?—to drop off my package, and almost got yourself killed in the process? Because I had to force myself and my silly headache out of bed for an hour to pick up my best friend, who's incidentally planning to work a full shift on a broken leg? Yeah, sure, I'm the one who deserves sympathy here." I suddenly knew I was going to be sick, and not just from the smothering migraine. I sucked in deep, calming breaths, trying to focus on the license plate of the car in front of me and ignore the strobing flash of its turn signal.

"Never mind the ice cream shop." Alejandro's voice was low, but I was too far gone to read his tone. "Just take us home."

Six blocks closer. My body screamed in relief as I turned onto our street and inched into the parking spot with the faded 29, empty for once by some miracle. But just the thought of the two flights of exterior stairs was dizzying enough to send me stumbling for the bushes, where I lost the few crackers I'd downed on my way to the hospital and whatever was left of yesterday's lunch. Steadying myself with a hand on the wall, I finally made my way over to where Alejandro sat five steps up, out of the reach of the blinding sunlight.

"You ready to do this, hot shot?" I wasn't sure I'd legitimately be any help to him, but even just giving him a cushion to fall on would be something, and maybe take away some of the guilty sting.

Alejandro shook his head and motioned to the step. Waiting probably wasn't the best approach, but I couldn't muster up the will to argue. I sank down next to him and rested my head against the railing, and Alejandro held out my phone.

"Go back upstairs and sleep. Callie is coming to pick me up."

I buried my face in my arm, too worn out to hold back the tears any longer. Had it really come to this? Alejandro could push through the pain of a broken leg to be there for a coworker, and I couldn't even drive the full distance to drop him off, let alone offer to cover for him like I should have. I ought to find him a new roommate, one that wouldn't force him to watch every scent he brought into the house, make him keep his music confined to his earbuds, or be totally unavailable to help in an emergency on a schedule no one could predict.

"Your headaches are not silly." Alejandro spoke softly, his voice sad and serious. "I have seen what they do to you. How much worse they become when you try to fight them. I do not blame you for that. I could not. You should not blame yourself."

His words only tightened the miserable knot in my gut.

"If I'm such a weakling that I can't help a friend, then maybe I shouldn't have any."

"Weak?" The surprise in Alejandro's tone sounded genuine. "David, of course you are not weak. I admire your strength always."

"What?" Shock made the word too sharp, and my ears rang. I swallowed back the pain and forced my eyes open to meet the concern in Alejandro's. "You're kidding me, right? What on earth is strong in—this?" I gestured vaguely at myself, and Alejandro shook his head.

"You truly do not see it? How brave it is every day that you get up and try again? How you forgive and do not throw me from the house when I forget not to bring home leftovers from Mama Rosa's? How when the doctors give no cure, you choose to live in spite of the pain? I see how much it hurts you. How you want to do so much more. But you do not give up. You do not shut out your friends, even when life is hard. I treasure your friendship, David. So much. You should not be out of bed, but you heard I was hurt, and you came. You think this is weakness? I think it is strength. I will remember it when my leg complains later that you were right. I will try to be as strong as you."

"That's—" I couldn't speak around the lump in my throat for a minute. "You can't be serious. I'm your example? There's no way."

"You do not believe it? You do not think I have noticed when you get up and turn off the hall light yourself when it bothers you instead of making me? Or when you stop catching up to talk with me on the days you have so much to do? You are such a friend to me always. Why do you think I wanted to help you today?"

Was that truly how he saw those incidents? Equal to everything he'd done for me? The thought was too much for my throbbing head, and I pressed my eyes shut again.

"How did you even know? This one hadn't started when you left yesterday."

Alejandro chuckled softly.

"It is not hard, *amigo*. You did not snore."

"Wait, what?" I squinted over at him, and he grinned.

"You snore like—" He paused, reaching for an idiom, but finally gave it up with a shrug. "Like something very loud. But only when you sleep deeply. The headaches—you cannot sleep deeply with them. So I know."

Alejandro knew more of my patterns than I knew myself, apparently. Did that mean there was any chance he could be right about the rest?

A sharp honk from the parking lot spun my world in circles, and Alejandro winced.

"I will tell her to keep the noise down. You are okay to make it?" He glanced up the stairs, and I swallowed hard.

"Yeah. I'll make it. Are you sure you will?"

"I will make it, *amigo*. We will both make it together."

I wanted to nod, but my swimming head wouldn't have taken it kindly, so I gave him the bit of a smile I found I could scrape together instead.

"If you need to come home early, call. I'll be there—if I can."

"I know you will." Alejandro flashed a smile that shone like the sun but didn't burn my eyes as he scooted himself down the stairs, balanced on his crutches, and made his clumsy way to Callie's car.

The PROMISE

"Cass?"

Her brother's tone was insistent and protective in spite of its slight hesitation. The sound sent a shiver down Cassidy's spine, and she fixed her eyes on the bouquet in her hand. The plastic stems and tiny silk tufts of baby's breath steadied her, recalling her conversation with Gilbert.

"Fake flowers, Cassie? You don't see our love that way, do you?"

Her heart had hurt at the wistful sound in his tone, and she'd given him her most confident smile with her answer.

"Sure I do. Real flowers wilt, you know. These will stay forever."

"Cass, honey." Derek had let himself into the room and stood behind her. Cassidy didn't turn. "Cass." The plea was a whisper, and Derek's arms came around her.

Cassidy wanted to let herself sink against the heavy fabric of his dress blues, to cry out the fear and anguish that the last few hours had brought to the boiling point. But she couldn't. He'd see it as an admission of doubt. She remained stiff in his arms.

"Come on, honey." Derek's voice was soft and coaxing in her ear. "Let's get out of here. Let's go to dinner. Go to a movie. Or just go home. You can curl up on the couch and cry all over my shirt. Okay?"

Cassidy shook her head stiffly. The threat of tears was too real to make an answer.

"We can't stay here all night, Cass. Everyone's gone except the pastor and the ladies who are cleaning up." His arms tightened around her as he spoke the words she dreaded. "Honey, he's not coming."

"You don't know him, Derek." As hard as she tried, she couldn't keep the quiver from her voice.

"I've known him longer than you have, honey." Derek's tone had acquired a trace of steel. He let go of her shoulders and moved in front of her, tipping her chin up to face him. "A ring on your finger is no guarantee from Gilbert Roth. I warned you a long time ago."

"He's changed."

"He must have told a hundred girls he'd changed, Cass. Greener pastures—always greener pastures. And he's a coward. Always has been, even if he covers it with his smooth talk. I'd track him down and break his nose if I thought it'd do any good."

"It's not like that, Derek. I remember him in high school. I'm sure he was worse in college. But he's a

Christian now. You don't understand—can't understand—how that changes a person."

Cassidy's heart throbbed for a moment with a deeper, more familiar pain. If only Derek could accept the new life, the real change that came from knowing Jesus. She'd hoped Gilbert might show him. He'd been so different this last year while Derek had been deployed. But now—

The muscles in Derek's jaw tightened.

"I understand that it gives him a brand-new crop of innocent, trusting hearts to break. And when he comes back 'repentant,' some other girl'll be right there waiting to give him another chance. He's playing you all."

"He's different." The plastic flower stems trembled in her hand, and she tightened her grasp.

Derek sighed, and his shoulders slumped, then he straightened and gently grasped her arms.

"You need to let it go. He's not coming. Cry, scream—I don't care. Just let your heart break now, not one tiny piece at a time when it's been days and weeks and months and he's still not here."

Cassidy's eyes closed, and a single tear escaped the tightly-woven lashes. Derek pulled her head to his shoulder, and she trembled with the effort it took to keep more tears from following the first.

"Come on, Cass." Derek's tone was soft, hopeful, tender. "Let's go home."

Her iron rod of resolve was weakening fast. If Derek had known it, he would have lifted her in his arms and carried her out the door, severing it completely.

"He'll be here."

Derek sighed.

"It's almost seven o'clock. They have to shut up the church. You can't stay here all night."

"He'll be here." It was all she had left.

The rod had worn down to the width of a wire, and she could feel it bending with the weight of her own emotions and the pressure of Derek's hands on her back. She hoped her brother didn't sense it; two more loving words from him might snap it. She hoped Gilbert would never know how low her faith had ebbed.

Please, God, help me stand.

"Cass—" Derek's plea was interrupted by the banging of a door in the distance and a startled hum of voices from the other side of the wall. Cassidy moved toward the sound, and Derek followed with a sigh of relief.

The fellowship hall had been stripped of nearly all its festive color. The tables were stacked against one wall; the chairs sat in rows, ready for Sunday school. A handful of ladies stood wide-eyed and whispering in the corner. And near the door, leaning against the wall and moving slowly toward her—

"Gil!" Cassidy ran to the disheveled figure and clasped him in her arms, regardless of the bouquet in her hands or the pristine condition of her dress.

"Cassie. Cassie, I'm so sorry." Gilbert's voice was hoarse and choked, and his broad shoulders trembled in her grasp. Cassidy stepped back and swiftly took in the gauze that covered his hands and forehead, the smell of smoke that clung thickly around him, the torn and soot-streaked state of the rented tuxedo.

"Gil, sit down." She caught the leg of a nearby chair with her foot and drew it forward, pressing Gilbert into it. It settled on top of her long skirt, pinning her to his side, and she made no effort to free herself. Gilbert doubled over, coughing violently, and she reached a hand up to rub his arm and shoulder.

"Cassie—so sorry," he repeated between spasms. Someone pressed a glass of water into her hand, and she held it carefully to Gilbert's lips, watching with relief as his breathing eased. He raised his eyes to meet hers, full of pain and anguish.

"I know what—what they must've said—what you must've thought."

"Look at me, Gil." Cassidy edged back as far as the chair's hold would permit and spread her skirt in a cloud around her. Picking up the bouquet that had fallen from her hand, she laid it in his lap. "Look at me. I'm still here. Still dressed. Still waiting. You promised, and you came. That's all that matters."

"Cassie." Gilbert's voice broke on the word, and she wrapped her arms around him and held him close again.

"Forgive me, ma'am."

Cassidy turned her head toward the strange voice without loosening her hold.

"I'm afraid it's ruined your day, and I'm terribly sorry, but I can't—can't entirely regret it. He saved my son's life."

Cassidy laid her head down on Gilbert's shoulder, unable to speak.

"What happened?" Derek spoke for the first time since they'd left her room.

"House caught fire. Wife and I weren't there. Babysitter got the two oldest out, but my little boy was asleep upstairs. He was driving along the road, saw the smoke, flames. Somehow got in and got to him. Part of the roof fell in, but he shielded my boy with his own body, and by then, the firemen were there. Got them both out."

Gilbert's shoulders shuddered slightly, and Cassidy rubbed gentle circles into them with her palms.

"When was this?" Derek's tone was unreadable.

"Around ten this morning. Live about fifteen minutes this side of Redmond. They took him to the hospital, patched him up, but he wouldn't stay after he could stand on his own feet, and they couldn't keep him. Seemed like he shouldn't be driving, so I brought him along. Least I could do—after everything he did."

Derek was silent, and Cassidy's heart glowed with joy. Even her brother couldn't argue the fact that Gilbert had been on his way to the church after picking up his tuxedo in Redmond. And his reputation as a coward—surely no one would ever dare call him that again.

Praise God, she hadn't given in. Gilbert was worth all her trust and more.

Derek's hand settled on her shoulder.

"Best get him back to a hospital, Cass. Smoke inhalation's nothing to play around with."

Cassidy nodded and raised her head, running a hand through Gilbert's soot-blackened hair.

"Is Pastor Blake still here?"

"Right here, Cassidy." He must have left his office to investigate the noise.

"Will you marry us, Pastor? Now?"

"Cassie." Gilbert's hoarse voice pulled her eyes back to his face. "This isn't how I wanted it. You should have—your dream wedding. The flowers. The guests. Not like—like this."

"Are you backing out of marrying my sister, Roth?" Derek's eyes narrowed, but there was an unexpected gentleness in his tone. Gilbert straightened.

"No. Never. I—"

"It's not the flowers and the guests I want, Gil," Cassidy interrupted before he could wear himself out with protests. "It's you. Marry me. Today. Now. Just like we planned."

Gilbert struggled to his feet and balanced himself with one hand on the back of a chair.

"I'd marry you anywhere—any time, Cassie Gray. And don't you—forget it."

Pastor Blake came to stand in front of them. Derek took hold of Cassidy's hand and placed it carefully on top of Gilbert's bandaged one, just as he would have in the formal ceremony. Before stepping back, he leaned close to her ear.

"You were right on this one, Cass. I'll watch and see about the rest."

"Your blessing?" Cassidy tilted her head to look into her brother's eyes. He shook his head slowly, but a smile tugged at the corner of his mouth.

"You and Gilbert Roth. Never thought I'd see the day." Leaning over again, he kissed her hair and nodded. "My blessing, Cass. You've got it."

GRIT

Rob gritted his teeth and willed his tired legs to keep pedaling. Only two more miles. Just two and he would be home. It had been the longest day of his life. Joining the gang for a bike ride to the ocean had seemed like a fun idea. Only he hadn't stopped to ask how long of a ride it was. But he had made it. At least this far. Couldn't he make the last two miles? The other guys were all up ahead and when one shouted something back, he nodded and waved.

"I wonder what he said," he mused as they disappeared around a bend in the road. "I hope it wasn't important."

His legs burned as he steered his bike toward the turn, feeling like he was moving by inches. Two miles. Less than two miles. Not much less, but still. He had to make it. If the guys started thinking they had to treat him gently, it would be the end of the easy friendship he'd basked in since moving to the little coastal town two months before.

And Phil. Rob's already red face flushed hotter at the thought of his brother. Phil had said he couldn't do it, had tried to convince Mom not to let him go. He wouldn't give Phil the satisfaction of seeing him come into town on the back of another boy's bike. He'd make it on his own if it killed him. Of course, Phil had been convinced it'd do just that.

Not strong enough. He was so tired of being not strong enough. It'd been six months since he'd been released from the hospital. Would Phil ever see him as strong enough? Two miles. Less than two. He was going to make it. He had to.

As he rounded the turn, Rob saw the rest of the group in the distance. How had they gained so quickly? They must be racing. It wouldn't be the first time today. They'd stop and wait for him eventually.

He'd slowed too much watching the cloud of dust and wheels ahead of him, and his bike began to wobble. Rob jerked the handlebars and gave one quick kick to the pedals, and the front wheel veered sharply toward a large rock. He grabbed for the brakes, but it was too late. The bike bucked, twisted, and rolled into the deep gully that bordered the road, landing on top of him at the bottom in a tangle of arms, legs, rocks, and spokes.

For a moment, Rob lay half stunned, then he slowly raised himself on his elbow. With a good deal of effort, he managed to pry himself apart from the bike and sit up. The gully spun around him, and he grabbed a nearby rock to keep himself upright.

As the world settled a little, Rob became aware of a dull pounding in his head and raised his hand to find something warm and wet trickling from a cut just below his hairline. He started to lift his other hand, but a sharper stab of pain revealed a larger, faster-bleeding gash on his right arm. He pulled his sleeve down over his shoulder and used his left hand to hold it against the cut as he glanced down at his legs. The left one was scratched and bruised, and his ankle throbbed a bit when he moved it. His right knee was scraped raw and covered in blood.

His eyes slid to his bike, and he winced. He was in no condition to ride, but the bent front wheel would make even walking the bike an awful task in his current state. Rob leaned his head against the side of the gully and closed his eyes as he waited for the bleeding to slow. He mentally traced the route they had followed that morning—no houses until the dirt road merged with the end of Main Street. How long would it take the boys to come looking for him? Or had that call he'd missed been a "see you tomorrow"? If they'd all gone home, he could sit here for hours without being found.

Rob groaned. He'd have given anything at that moment to be tucked under the soft, clean covers of his own bed, even if Mom's worried fussing and Phil's "I told you so" were part of the deal. If Phil would only show up now…

"I have to get home." He'd kept the self-pep talks inside his head all day, but saying them out loud made them seem truer, more real. "Someone's got to come along, but if they don't—I've just got to start. I won't get anywhere sitting here."

Rob checked the bleeding on his arm, which had slowed, then carefully inched himself out of the gully, dragging the bent bicycle by the handlebars with his feet. At the top, he tried to stand but gasped and sank back to the ground as his knee gave a sharp protest. Tears stung his eyes, and he buried his face in his good arm.

"This isn't getting me home." Hissing the words through clenched teeth, Rob staggered to his feet, ignoring the throbbing in his ankle and holding tightly to his thighs until the pain in his knee subsided a little. With some effort and more than one searing reminder of the cut in his arm, he got the bike upright and leaned against the handlebars. It actually wasn't a bad crutch, or wouldn't have been if the front wheel hadn't been so uncooperative. Still, it was better than nothing, or at least that's what he'd tell himself.

Rob bit back a cry at the pain in his knee as he began inching along the road. Two miles. A little less, but still—almost two miles. He'd been pushing to make it on a bike. But walking—and walking injured? The thought made him dizzy, and he turned his attention back to his feet. A painful step. An excruciating step. Stay upright when the bent wheel caught or twisted. Catch a breath when the throbbing dulled for an instant, then hold it for a fresh wave of pain. Looking up at the trees in the unattainable distance was torture, and after a few glances, he kept his eyes trained on the dirt road. Left foot. Grit teeth. Right foot. Breathe. One step more. Just one step more.

The pattern became his entire existence. It consumed him so completely that he barely registered the whine of a car motor until a door slammed with a thump.

"Robbie!"

Rob slowly lifted his gaze and collapsed into his brother's arms. It was a minute before he knew anything else, but when the fog began to clear, he found himself on the ground with Phil leaning over him, wiping his face with a wet handkerchief.

"Phil." The word was a sob, and Phil looked down quickly.

"Take it easy, Robbie. It'll all be okay. What happened?"

"Caught my wheel—on a rock. Crashed in the gully. Too far behind—no one saw." To his dismay, Rob found himself trembling all over. Phil held a canteen to his lips and lifted his head to help him drink, then went to work tending his cuts with the first-aid kit he always carried. He talked softly as he worked.

"I saw the boys at Marco's, and Gary told me they'd raced the last mile and a half. They were waiting for you, but I told them I'd meet you and send you straight home to supper. I didn't think you'd want them to see if you'd given out."

"You were right, Phil." Rob closed his eyes, and his shoulders slumped, then tensed again as Phil touched his knee.

"Right about what?"

"I wasn't strong enough. I couldn't make it. I shouldn't have—" Rob couldn't keep back a grunt of pain as Phil applied an alcohol wipe to the scrape. "I shouldn't have tried."

Phil didn't answer until he'd wrapped the knee in gauze and cleaned a couple of smaller cuts. Finally, his eyes met Rob's.

"Robbie, I've never been so wrong in my life."

Rob blinked at him dully.

"About what?"

"Lots of things. But mostly about you." He moved to sit near Rob's head again and carefully stroked his brother's hair back from his face. "I was so scared, Robbie. All that time you were in the hospital, and then afterwards—I've never been so scared in my life. All I could think was that we'd lose you—and I couldn't do anything to stop it." Phil swallowed hard, and Rob wondered if there were really tears in his eyes, or if it was just a trick of the sun. Phil went on talking quietly.

30

"When you started to get better—I couldn't let go of that fear. I just wanted to hide you away where nothing could hurt you ever again."

"That doesn't sound so bad," Rob murmured. The tension was draining from his body, and Phil's gentle stroking of his hair had nearly put him to sleep.

"No, Robbie." Phil's voice was quiet, but his words had a ring that made Rob's eyes open wide. "That would have been the worst mistake of my life. You're not one of Mom's porcelain figurines that needs to be wrapped in cotton and stuck on a shelf. You're stronger than that—much stronger—and I can see that now. Taking your life away to protect you—it'd hurt you much worse than anything else could."

"But I'm not strong, Phil." Rob felt his lip trembling. "You were right; the ride was too long. I was beat—a long time before I fell."

"Beat, but not licked."

"Huh?"

"Where'd you fall, Robbie?"

"Just after the turn."

"So you made over eighteen miles of a twenty-mile round trip on your bike, when I didn't think you'd last ten. And you would have made the rest if you hadn't hit that rock."

"How do you know that?"

"Because I found you half a mile from that spot, limping on a bad knee and not an overly good ankle and pushing a bent bicycle, that's how." Phil tipped Rob's chin up and looked into his eyes. "You've got grit, kid. Right-down, pure, unadulterated grit. And when those cuts heal up, you're going to prove it by biking out to Pickett's Gorge with me."

Rob caught his breath. He'd heard so much about Pickett's Gorge, and to go there with Phil— He broke off the train of thought and shook his head.

"That's a fifteen-mile ride one way. I'd never make the whole thing, even if I wasn't still stiff and sore."

"We'll wait 'til the soreness is past. And we'll take it in easy stages—camp there a couple nights instead of coming straight home. Are you game?"

For answer, Rob wrapped his better arm around his brother and held on tightly.

"You can look out for me any time, Phil."

"I plan to. You're a special kid, Robbie. But I don't aim to be the one that rubs your grit off."

"I wouldn't mind getting rid of some of it." Rob brushed at the coating of dirt that covered his skin, and Phil laughed.

"The outer stuff we can take care of. Just don't let anyone steal it from your heart." In another minute, he'd swept Rob off the ground and into the car. "Let's get you home, hero. What do you say?"

"I say I love you, Phil." Rob smiled and closed his eyes as he lay back against the seat. "And if you're really taking me out to Pickett's Gorge, then I'd say I'm not the only one who's brave."

"Maybe you've taught me something." Phil reached over and stroked his brother's hair again before putting the car in gear. And under the whine of the motor, Rob was certain he heard, "And I love you, too, kid."

FISH TEARS
A LOVE BLIND PREQUEL

I couldn't believe I was crying. Over a goldfish.

I crammed my fists into my eyes, hoping to squeeze hard enough to turn off the tears and erase the evidence that they'd ever been there. When it didn't work, I sank to the floor and buried my face in my knees, trying to hold my breath so my shoulders wouldn't shake.

Even girls didn't cry over goldfish.

I remembered exactly how Ashlynn Jones had described her dead goldfish to our first-grade class, her grin getting wider and wider as she moved from what it'd looked like when they found it to the way it'd flopped and turned circles when her dad flushed it down the toilet. I had laughed along with the others because that's what boys did when they were grossed out. The girls had all squealed and covered their ears, except a couple that still liked being grossed out as much as the boys. Our teacher, Miss Kline, had looked sort of sick and made us line up for lunch early instead of letting us ask questions like she usually did.

But she hadn't cried. Nobody had—not even Ashlynn.

I was a boy. Nine years old now, and in fourth grade. I shouldn't be crying. Not over this. But I couldn't stop, and it scared me.

"Hey, Jake?"

The little voice came from the bedroom door—the one I hadn't shut when I came in to feed Orange Peel. There was no way she wouldn't see me and no way I could pretend I hadn't been crying. I didn't look up.

"Hey, Jake, Mommy took Sef to soccew pwactice, and Daddy said I can do bubbles. Wanna come?"

I didn't have to open my eyes to picture Mellie standing in the doorway to Seth's room, her yellow curls bouncing up and down as she rocked back and forth on her feet. Mellie was only six and still couldn't say her brother's name right, let alone anything with an r. If she saw me crying, she'd probably run for her dad, and there was no way I wanted Mr. Clair to know.

I opened my mouth to say no, but the second I stopped holding my breath, my words broke in a sob. The next minute, Mellie had her arms around my neck and was hugging me tight.

I don't know why it worked, but some way that hug seemed to let loose a big lump in my chest, and after a couple more sobs I'd already been holding in, the tears ran faster but didn't sting so bad.

"Awe you sad about youw mommy and daddy?" Mellie whispered in my ear, and I shook my head and tried to stretch my short sleeves far enough to wipe my eyes. Mom and Dad had gone on a business trip, leaving me with my best friend's family for a week, but they were coming back, so it would have been silly to cry about them.

Almost as silly as crying over a goldfish.

"What's wong?" Mellie's arms tightened around my neck, and her soft hair pressed up against my ear.

I shouldn't tell her. Even six-year-old girls didn't cry over goldfish. But she just stood there holding onto me like she wasn't planning to let go, so I swallowed hard and pointed.

Mellie let go of my neck, and I lifted my head and watched her walk to the dresser and stretch up on her toes to see better. After a minute, she turned, eyes wide.

"Owange Peel can swim upside down?"

I shook my head, swallowing something that felt like a golf ball in my throat.

"He's—he's dead." With the words came more tears. I tried to brush them away but only made my cheeks wetter.

Mellie left the fishbowl and sat down next to me on the floor, leaning her head against my arm but not taking her eyes off the fish.

"Why did he die?"

"I don't know." The words opened up an aching corner of my heart that I'd been afraid to let myself think about. I'd forgotten to feed him one day last week. The bowl had wobbled a little yesterday when Seth slammed the bedroom door. Was the air at the Clairs' house a little colder than mine? I was afraid to ask a grown-up, but Mellie wouldn't know anyway. "Maybe—maybe I didn't feed him enough. Maybe I didn't take care of him right. Maybe coming here made him sick."

"But you take good cawe of him, Jake!" Mellie's little voice sounded angry at the idea. "And coming hewe didn't make him sick befowe."

She was right, and I breathed a little bit better. I'd forgotten Seth and his family had taken care of Orange Peel when we went to visit Grandpa a few months ago. And I'd also forgotten to feed him the day I'd taken him home. So it couldn't have been those things that killed him now.

Thinking of Grandpa made my tears start again. I'd known all along why losing Orange Peel hurt so bad. He hadn't just been my pet. He'd been my last Christmas present from Grandpa—maybe the last one ever.

Mom said Grandpa was dying—that our visit this summer might be the last time I got to see him. If Grandpa died, I'd never get to walk with him again, never hear him tell me stories, never feel his scratchy beard on my cheek when he hugged me. And now I wouldn't even have Orange Peel to remember him with. I put my head down on my knees again. Mellie kept her head against my arm.

"Owange Peel was a good fishie," Mellie said quietly after a minute. "He had a vewy pwetty tail."

I swallowed and felt something wobbly that might have wanted to be a smile pricking the corners of my mouth.

"He—he always ate his food really fast. Like, one second it was there, and then boom! Gone. Like I'd never even fed him."

"I liked when I put my face by him and he came ovew and looked at me." Mellie sighed, and I put my arm around her.

"I liked that, too."

"What do fishies do aftew they'we dead?" Mellie looked up at me with big, trusting eyes, and I shuddered a little.

"I think—you're supposed to—to flush them in the toilet."

I waited for Mellie's eyes to get big and grossed out, but she just looked at me for a minute like she was thinking, then nodded.

"I guess they like to stay in the watew."

I knew Orange Peel wouldn't be liking anything anymore, but for some reason, the idea of leaving him safe in the water made my heart not hurt quite so bad.

Mellie's lips suddenly wobbled, and her eyes filled with tears.

"If we flush him, we can't evew see him again."

I shook my head, and a couple new tears rolled out the corners of my eyes.

"I can't keep him if he's dead, though. He'll get—nasty and gross-looking—and won't be any fun."

Mellie nodded and grabbed my hand.

"Can I say bye to him?"

I nodded hard and had to wipe my cheeks on my collar, since I was out of dry spaces on my sleeves. I stood next to Mellie as she pushed herself up on her tiptoes at Seth's dresser and watched Orange Peel not moving for a long minute. Finally, she said, "Bye, Owange Peel. You wewe a good fishie," then turned and threw her arms around my neck and buried her face in my chest. I could feel the wet spots her tears made on my shirt, and I wondered if she could feel the ones mine were making in her hair.

"You want to help me?" I asked finally, and Mellie nodded. I carefully lifted the fishbowl and carried it to the bathroom, then set it on the side of the tub and looked down at it for a long time. "Bye, Orange Peel," I said finally, not even minding that Mellie could hear my voice cracking. "You were a good fish." I wiped my eyes again so I could see, then I dumped the whole fishbowl into the toilet and, without letting myself think, pushed the handle. Then I sank down on the floor and

40

cried, not sobbing like I had at first but letting the tears quietly start and stop and start again until I was worn out. Mellie had disappeared somewhere, and I finally pushed myself up, returned the empty fishbowl to its place on Seth's dresser, laid down on my sleeping bag, and closed my stinging eyes.

I wasn't sure how long I'd been there before a little hand on my shoulder made me look up. Mellie was kneeling next to me, blinking down at me with one hand behind her back.

"I made somefing fow you, Jake. So you won't be lonely 'til you get a new fishie."

I almost told her I didn't want another fish, but she held something out toward me, and I took it without a word.

It was only a piece of blue construction paper with a lopsided fish shape done in orange crayon. But at least I could tell it was a fish, and I wondered how many tries it had taken her to get it right. At the top of the page, she'd written "Jaks fisy" in big letters, the J backwards as usual. And suddenly, I knew I did want another fish. It wouldn't be Orange Peel, but it would remind me of him—and Grandpa—and that would be enough. I looked at the paper for a long minute, then stood up and propped it against the empty fishbowl.

"Thanks, Mellie."

"You wanna do bubbles?"

"Yeah." My voice cracked just a little as she slipped her hand into mine. "Well, I mean, I'm kinda tired. But I'll watch you."

Mellie's face lit up, and she pulled me out to the porch where Mr. Clair had set up the bubble maker. I turned it on and sat on the steps, leaning against the rail while I watched Mellie chase and catch the shining bubbles that swam and broke in the breeze. And somehow, I didn't feel so bad anymore—even if I had just been crying over a goldfish.

The Deal

Landon was so dead.

Nate Harper did his best to ignore the gawking pedestrians that lined the slushy sidewalks. Not that he blamed them; he'd have stared hard enough if it had been some other poor sap waddling through the business district like an oversized goose in a snorkel mask, flippers, and a full business suit, struggling to hold up the giant pool tube strapped around his middle.

So incredibly dead.

Any other day, he could imagine himself laughing when the scene was over, giving Landon bonus points for creativity, even texting a picture to Grayson to make him smile. But his jerk of a roommate had kicked the embarrassment factor up to eleven by choosing the biggest day of his professional career to call their "friendly" deal. At least the ridiculous flippers hadn't dumped him in the slush—yet—but he'd seriously overestimated how fast he'd be able to walk in them, and his chances of getting into the Forsythe building without anyone but the receptionist noticing were quickly dwindling to nothing.

If he missed this appointment, Landon was worse than dead.

Sucking in a breath that tasted like foggy plastic, Nate forged ahead, keeping his eyes on the gleaming glass doors of the Forsythe building that finally loomed into view around the corner. He hiked the pool tube higher and shot a quick glance at his watch, panic surging in his chest as the numbers registered.

This wasn't funny anymore. Not the least little bit.

Bouncing and flopping his way through the jostling crowd, he finally reached the steps, only to discover that the architect hadn't designed them to accommodate a man in flippers. Inexcusable, really—if you were building a dolphin tank.

Nate turned sideways and shuffled up the steps, then folded his body like an acrobat to fit the tube into the revolving door. The pressure shot him out like a cannon on the other end, the flippers finally losing traction and landing him on his rear a good three feet down the polished marble floor.

Rising awkwardly to his feet with the hindrance of the flippers, Nate raised his head to find every eye in the spacious lobby trained on him, some of their owners still paused in the act of whatever they'd been doing when he burst onto the scene. With a fervent prayer that Oliver Rawson was not among them, he made a beeline for the men's room and divested himself of the swim gear with record speed, slipping on the shoes he'd carried in a drawstring backpack and allowing himself one quick swipe at his hair and a violent shake of his jacket that he could only hope smoothed a few of the wrinkles. Then he squared his shoulders and reentered the lobby, approaching the blond woman waiting at the desk as though he were any normal businessman, not the source of the strangest aberration in the entire history of the Forsythe building.

"Nathan Harper. I have an appointment with Mr. Rawson."

"Indeed you do." Nate turned with a start to see a gentleman with salt-and-pepper hair and a silver-pinstriped suit, who most certainly *had* been standing just there when he'd made his grand entrance, motioning toward a plush conference room on the other end of the lobby.

His shoes should have been comfortably familiar after the unwieldy flippers, but every step felt weighted with lead as Nate followed the older man into the room and took the indicated seat at the table. Oliver Rawson sat in the chair across from him and rested his arms on the polished surface, tilting his head just slightly in a manner that Nate took as his cue to proceed. Sucking in a deep breath in an attempt to force the rest of the morning from his mind, he plunged into the pitch he had so carefully prepared.

"Mr. Rawson, I believe my company's services would be of great benefit to Forsythe, Rawson, and Caldwell in this new venture you intend to explore. While it's true that we don't have the experience of some in the space, you'll find that our innovative approach and cutting-edge methods mean that we view problems from a fresh perspective and can often exploit angles that are overlooked by the more established players. And with our reduced overhead..."

Mr. Rawson allowed him to make it to the middle of his second paragraph before he lifted a hand.

"Very well, Mr. Harper; you've proved that you can keep your cool under pressure. I've read your pitch and seen your portfolio; it's why you're sitting here today. However, I don't think we'll make any real headway until we address the elephant—or was it a giant duck?—in the room."

Nate swallowed hard as the heat began to creep up his neck.

"Yes, sir. That was—extremely unprofessional. I beg your pardon."

"Part of your company's 'innovative approach'?"

"No, sir." Panic welled as Nate realized for the first time just what this ridiculous stunt could mean to the reputation of his company and the prospects of the rest of his team. He fought the urge to squeeze the bridge of his nose, balling his hands into fists instead. "That had nothing to do with the company or this interview."

46

Nothing except that Landon had purposely timed it for maximum embarrassment, with no concern for what would happen to anyone else if their little start-up went down in flames. "It was a—a personal matter. A very badly advised deal I made with a friend."

"A bet?"

"Of sorts. I don't gamble, but—yes, the effect was the same. You're familiar with the Sally Kuyper Bikea-thon?"

"Of course. The firm sponsors it every year."

"Yes, sir." How could he have forgotten that? "Well, I challenged my roommate to a contest for who could raise the most money this year. Thought I had a good chance until the day of the ride, when I found out he used to race BMX in high school." Of course Landon had purposely withheld that information. But Nate had contented himself with the thought that all the money had gone to a good cause. At least until today.

"And the loser had to…" Oliver Rawson's expression was completely unreadable. Nate forced himself to keep his shoulders straight as he offered a stiff attempt at a smile.

"Wear a costume of the other's choosing at a place and time of the other's choosing, with no backing out for any reason." Come to think of it, maybe Landon had been merciful, after a fashion. Just the thought of sitting in this meeting still wearing the mask and flippers, not to mention the plastic tube, was enough to make him break out in hives.

"Whose idea was this?"

"Mine, sir. Both the contest and the penalty, unfortunately."

"I believe that's called being hoist by your own petard." The faintest glint of amusement seemed to light Mr. Rawson's face for just an instant. "Well, Mr. Harper, what would the conditions have been for your poor friend, had he not had the good fortune to race BMX in high school?"

Nate bit his lips together and blinked hard as he focused his eyes out the window, trying not to dwell on the picture of Grayson's wasted little face.

"I have a—a cousin in the cancer ward. That's why I do the bikeathon every year. It sounds ridiculous, but—well, my roommate could double for Superman—at least in the latest movies—and Gray's got a serious superhero obsession. It would make the kid's whole life, but Landon can't stand the resemblance and won't do it without some kind of a major shove. This was the closest I've come—so far."

"Do I judge that you don't intend to let it go, then?"

Forgetting himself for an instant, Nate snorted.

"After today? He's going down so hard..." He caught himself and snapped back to the present as Mr. Rawson rose from the table.

"I believe I've seen everything I need to, Mr. Harper. I won't waste any more of your time."

He should have known better than to come. He should have just kept walking in those ridiculous flippers, waddled right past the door without looking back. It would have been better than embarrassing his whole company this way.

"Can you have a contract on my desk next week?"

The words cut jarringly into the apology Nate was composing for the amazing team that had taken a chance on him, the team he had just let down in the worst way imaginable.

"Sir?"

"We'd like to get this venture off the ground as quickly as possible, and of course our legal team will need some time to look things over. How quickly can you get us a contract?"

"I—" Sylvia could have the contract written up tomorrow, but the words clogged in his throat. "Do you mean—" He had to pull himself together. Act like a professional. Not botch this any more than he already had. But what on earth? "We can—you'll have it by next week, yes, sir."

"Good." Oliver Rawson crossed to the door and put his hand on the knob, then glanced over at Nate. This time there was no mistaking the twinkle in his eye. "Any questions for me, Mr. Harper?"

"We didn't even discuss—the project."

"As I said, I've seen your ideas. I don't deny that they're impressive, or that they have a certain spark that sets them apart from most of the other applicants. But what I wanted out of today was a sense of your character—to know that your values fit the standard Forsythe, Rawson, and Caldwell has always striven to uphold."

"But shouldn't you ask me—those questions?"

"I don't see why. From what I've learned here, you're a man who takes pride in his work, stands true to his word, and doesn't retreat in the face of a serious setback. You're creative, tenacious, loyal, and honest, not to mention civic-minded, all without taking yourself too seriously. And may I assume that you've learned your lesson about open-ended agreements?"

"Absolutely." Nate tried not to choke on the lump in his throat, and the smile in Mr. Rawson's eyes tugged at the corners of his mouth.

"Then I don't see anything more to ask, do you? Have the contract on my desk next week."

Oliver Rawson strode out the door, leaving Nate standing speechless in the empty conference room. Was it somehow remotely possible that God had just used the greatest embarrassment of his life to land him the deal of his dreams? Swallowing hard, Nate straightened his tie and retraced his steps to where he'd left the bits of his costume. Odd that no one had stolen them—if it were a public pool.

Stuffing the mask and flippers into the backpack as best he could, Nate slung it over his shoulders and picked up the tube. As he strode back through the lobby, snickers wafted his way from the reception desk, and when he glanced back, the blonde quickly hid her face behind a folder.

Landon was still so dead.

ONLY A TREASURE

Dense ferns and tangled vines choked my path as I stumbled away from the light of the campfire. No one called after me, but the raucous laughter quieted, no doubt at a look or a word from Mattan. They all knew why I had gone, which made my attempt to hide it useless, but the bare thought of an audience made my stomach roll harder. I clapped a hand to my mouth and pushed on until the murmur of voices faded, then dropped to my knees and lost the last of the morning's scanty breakfast at the base of a moss-covered tree.

When my stomach slowly retreated from my throat, I covered the mess with shaking fingers, then crept to the other side of the tree and leaned back against it, letting the damp moss cool my burning cheek. It wasn't even a full minute later that I heard a carefully placed step behind me, and Lanz's arm settled around my shoulders.

"How did you find me?" I didn't open my eyes.

"You don't exactly try to hide your trail."

Not to mention that he could track the wind through the trees if he had reason to. I shivered in spite of the warm air, and Lanz pulled me a little closer.

"What would Meara say if she saw you walking on that leg?" If I kept talking, could I hold back the rush of tears that threatened? I had already proved myself soft enough for one day.

"That I'll cripple myself for life, most likely. And that she's glad I came after you."

The tears breached my feeble defenses, and I swiped helplessly at my cheeks.

"I'm such a weakling. I'll never be like the rest of you."

"That's not a bad thing with this group, Tsara." His voice held the grave, thoughtful note that made him special among all the warriors in camp. I huffed a sound that was meant to be a laugh, but it came out more of a moan.

"I'm no good even in the infirmary. I nearly fainted at the sight of Dass's arm today."

"*Dass* nearly fainted at the sight of his arm. I felt a bit queasy looking at it myself."

"Dass had lost more than a quart of blood. And you had refused any painkillers for your leg. I had no such excuse."

"You needed no excuse, *tesoro*."

Treasure. The pet name the entire camp had given me should have soothed, but today it stabbed. This was all I

54

was. A useless treasure. Something to be guarded and watched over, protected and defended, kept safe at all costs. Not capable of joining in the battle, of taking a blow for my friends, even of tending to their wounds.

"A fine treasure I am. Three dead, more than a dozen injured, Meara nearly run off her feet, and all I can do is make bandages."

"You think we didn't need those bandages? Or that Meara had time to make them herself?"

"You could have made them and stayed off that leg as you were supposed to if I hadn't been so weak. I'll never find a way to repay all you've given me. I can't even cook." I choked on a sob, feeling the absurdity but unable to prevent it.

"Your cooking is improving." Lanz couldn't hide the hint of humor in his voice, but his next words softened into tenderness again. "And you were never asked to repay us, *tesoro*. But I won't agree that you did nothing. Didn't you sing?"

"Oh, sing!" I batted the word away contemptuously, and Lanz's hand tightened on my shoulder.

"Yes, sing. You've never heard anything like the hush that fell over the infirmary when your voice floated through the canvas. We forget, Tsara. In the rush and roar of battle, we forget the truth you sing about. Sometimes we even forget why we fight. You remind us that there is an end. A greater purpose to this war. A future beyond the blood and pain."

55

I shivered again as the piles of bloody bandages rose before my eyes, and Lanz leaned his cheek against my hair.

"Forgive me, *tesoro*. I'm too hardened to it. All of us are. This is why we need you."

"Three years, Lanz." The words left my lips on a whisper. "Three years, and I've lost count of the battles. Why can't I harden? It would be better."

"No, Tsara." Lanz pulled back, and there was a ring of steel in his tone. "Never wish that. Never."

"Meara says the sight of blood turned her stomach when she first came. Now she doesn't even flinch."

"You are not Meara."

"I know it. Meara is far more useful."

Lanz was silent for a moment as he pulled me close again, and when he did speak, his words came slowly.

"More useful perhaps, in a strictly practical sense. But not more needed. Never more needed, *tesoro*."

"There, you see?" Tears filled my eyes as the faces of those who would never return floated through my mind. "You're warriors, all of you. I'm only a useless treasure, good for nothing except to be placed on a shelf and locked away from danger. I want to do something, Lanz! I owe you all so much."

"Oh, Tsara." His voice held pain, and I raised my still brimming eyes to his face. "How can you not see it? You *are* our treasure. This is why we need you." He lifted a hand to the knot of my hair and began carefully removing the pins that held the braided bun in place. "Do you still remember nothing of the day we found you?"

I shook my head and waited. I had heard the story many times, though never from Lanz, but nothing seemed able to pierce the darkness that shrouded it in my mind. I remembered nestling next to my sister beneath the roof of our family's home, then waking to an infirmary tent with Meara and Mattan bending over me. I could imagine the horrors that had come between—imagine, but never remember.

"You were lying among the dead." Lanz's voice sounded far away, as though he was standing again amid the ruins of my village. "You were pale and still as death, but something—a breath, a flutter, I never knew just what—made me look closer. When I found that you were alive…" He was silent a moment as he removed the last pin and began loosing the twists of my braid. "It was like finding a pool in the desert, or a flower growing from a bed of rock. You were there and alive amid all the destruction. So innocent. So beautiful."

He finished freeing the long, dark curls that were such a hindrance to everything when I forgot to tie them back, but that I hadn't been able to bring myself to cut short like Meara's. Always before, the story had been "we"—"when we found you," "when we brought you back." Had I even known that it had been Lanz at the first?

"You became very precious to us that day, *tesoro*. You reminded us that there was still beauty amid the ashes, that there was life in the midst of death. Even now, when you pale at the sight of a wound or sicken at the dark humor we use to cloak our grief, you remind us of what we fight for—the women and children, yes and even the men, who should never have such horrors brought to their doors." Lanz tilted my chin to look into my eyes once more. "When we look at you, our hearts say, 'Here is our Tsara. She has seen so much that she was never meant to see, and yet she is still filled with beauty and truth.' But if you were to harden, our hearts would say, 'What's the use? Even our Tsara could not stand against the darkness. Why should we try?'"

I was crying now, tears that were unlike any I ever remembered, and Lanz's eyes shone wet in the faint moonlight that filtered through the thick canopy above us.

"We need you, *tesoro*. We need you more than we need another warrior, or even another nurse. We fight for you, for your future and ours. Never say that our treasure is worthless. It means more to us than you can ever know."

I wrapped my arms around him and held him hard, and he returned the embrace more firmly than ever before. We stayed that way for a long moment, then I pulled back and met his eyes again.

"What can I do, Lanz? How can I help? Now. Tonight."

"Come back and sing for us, Tsara. The rough joking only covers our wounds. Your hymns are the balm that heals."

I ducked my head and nodded, then scrambled to my feet and steadied Lanz's arm as he pushed stiffly to his.

"Let me look at that leg when we return to camp."

"There's no need."

"You're in pain, and Meara has enough work on her hands. Please let me, Lanz. If I stop trying and sit idle, I won't be a treasure worth having. Let me do what I can."

"All right, *tesoro*. I'll admit it does hurt tonight." His arm settled around my shoulders again as we began picking our way through the dense ferns and tangled vines, back to the light of the campfire.

Made in the USA
Columbia, SC
17 August 2022

64827814R00037